LEON AND ASHA VS THE ALIENS

LEON AND ASHA VS THE ALIENS

Naomi Jones

Illustrated by
Leo Trinidad

Collins

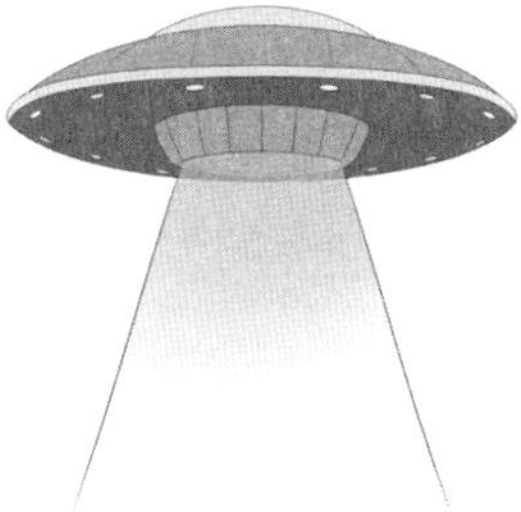

Chapter 1

"Goal!" Asif shouted, before doing a victory dance across the pitch.

"You'd think he'd never scored a goal before." Asha rolled her eyes as she sat down on a bench next to her best friend Leon. "Roxy's always going on about how she's actually a *much* better player than Asif, but everyone thinks he's better 'cause he makes such a fuss when he scores."

"Uh-huh," Leon said. He was drawing a dragon with razor-sharp teeth and a wicked smile in his sketchbook. He was trying to make sure he got the dragon's wings just right and was wondering what colour they should be.

"Are you listening?" Asha asked, with a frown.

"Yup. Roxy's being annoying, and so is Asif. They're both obsessed with football."

Asha sighed. That did *kind* of sum it up. Roxy was Asha's twin sister. They looked identical, right down to their matching afros and the smattering of freckles across their nose. But that was where the similarities ended. Roxy was obsessed with football. She liked to play it, watch it and talk about it endlessly. Asha loved books, especially fantasy ones or graphic novels. Her favourite things to do were read, write her own stories or talk about books (as long as the books had nothing to do with football). She was going to be an author when she was older.

"So, I've had an idea for Dee." Asha pulled a notebook out of her bag.

"Dee?" Leon lifted his pen off the page and pushed up his glasses to look at her properly for the first time. "Who's Dee?"

"The dragon," Asha said, pointing at Leon's sketchbook. "Remember, you said you'd started drawing a dragon character and I said I'd have a think about what their story could be."

"Oh yeah," Leon smiled, and ran his hands through his scruffy brown hair.

Most of the kids in their class spent breaktimes playing football, but Asha and Leon used them to create their own graphic novels.

Asha started telling Leon about the idea she'd had for Dee, a friendly, funny dragon who lived in a world filled with other, much fiercer dragons until she accidentally fell through a portal and ended up in their world. Dee wanted to get home but discovered most people were too scared of dragons to help her, apart from a boy named Max.

"I like it," Leon said.

Just then, a dark shadow fell over the playground. They both looked up and watched as the sky turned from light blue to grey to black in a matter of minutes.

"Weird," Asha said, as the wind picked up and hail began to fall in sharp, icy drops.

"Quick!" Leon and Asha gathered up their things and joined everyone else as they ran for their classroom door.

Roxy and Asif were the last inside. They'd stayed out playing football in the hail until the last possible second.

Asha rolled her eyes again. Her sister's arms were red from where the hail had stung her. Roxy untied her school jumper from her waist and put it on, shivering slightly but still smiling.

"OK, everyone," Miss Meswania told them. "It's just a little hail. Let's settle down and open our Maths books."

It took a few minutes for the hail to stop and the excited chatter to drop to a rumbling murmur, before Miss Meswania started explaining what they were doing. Leon tried to concentrate, but he always found it hard to remember everything his teachers said.

He could hear Roxy and Asif whispering behind him.

Priya, who was sitting nearby, whispered, "They never stop talking about football, do they?"

Leon smiled and asked her what they were supposed to be doing.

Once Priya explained, he began to copy down

the sums on the board but, halfway through, he realised he'd accidentally written some of the numbers down in the wrong order. He knew it was because of his dyslexia, but it did seem ironic that an accountant's son could be so bad at maths. He doodled a cute kitten pouncing on the sums instead.

"Miss," Asif said after a moment. "The sky's purple."

"I can see that," said their teacher. "Just ignore what's happening outside please and concentrate on your work."

Leon looked outside the window. The sky was now a bright, vivid purple, like a neon bruise.

He elbowed Asha next to him. "Look," he hissed. "It's really weird."

Asha wrinkled her nose. "It looks like Avaria."

"What?" Leon whispered back.

"It's the magical kingdom in the book I'm reading."

“I know the sky looks strange,” said Miss Meswania, when it became clear most of the class was also looking out of the window and not doing maths. “But I’m sure there’s a perfectly reasonable explanation.”

For a minute or two, there was a quiet, studious kind of silence as everyone turned back to their books. Leon could feel everyone around him working. He wished, not for the first time, that he found schoolwork as easy as everyone else.

Then the peace was broken by the sound of the chair next to him being pushed back. "Woah!" Priya gasped, as she stood up.

Leon lifted his head at the note of panic in her voice. Priya was pointing to the window where a wide beam of bright, white light was shooting out from behind one of the purple clouds. It ended in a spotlight on their playground.

All the kids in Leon's class ran over to the window.

"It's probably nothing," said Miss Meswania, but she didn't sound sure at all.

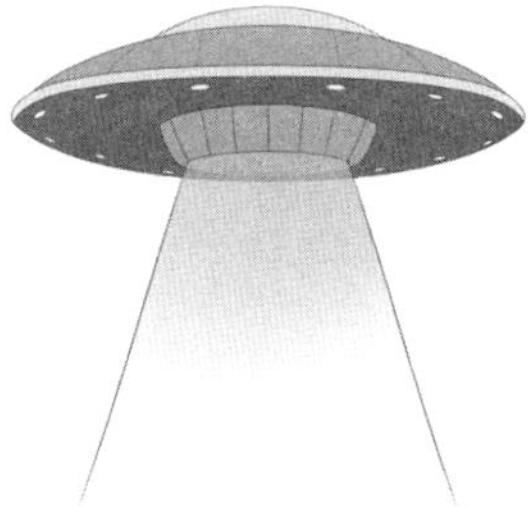

Chapter 2

It wasn't nothing. A few seconds later, something appeared in the beam of light from behind the dark clouds. It was large, round and silver. The closer it got to the playground, the brighter the beam of light became.

Leon and Asha shaded their eyes with their hands. Everyone in class did the same.

"What is it?" Asif said, squinting beneath his hands.

"It looks like a spaceship," Priya replied.

"But ... it can't be," said Miss Meswania.

"Woah," said Asha, as the round, silver

object landed with a thump so loud it made their classroom shake.

Leon grabbed his sketchbook from his desk.

He could hear Miss Meswania phoning Mr King, their head teacher, to tell him something big had landed outside their window.

Asha just stood there, eyes wide as Roxy came and stood next to her.

"Do you think it could be – " Asha asked.

"Aliens?" Roxy finished her sentence.

"No, maybe, I don't know," Asha replied. She couldn't take her eyes off it.

Leon's pen flew over the paper as the bright beam of light dimmed. He tried to capture the curves of the sleek metal. He couldn't see any wings or wheels; there were no windows or doors. It was just a completely round, smooth, circular silver object, about the width of a lorry.

"What else could it be?" Roxy asked her sister.

"A super-secret government experiment?" Asha suggested. "Creatures from another dimension?"

"You read too much," Roxy said.

"There's no such thing," Asha replied.

"We should go take a look." Asif opened the door that led to the playground and stepped outside. Some of the other kids from their class jostled forwards, pushing each other to get outside quicker. Leon hung back with Asha – they were the last to follow everyone out. In one hand, he clutched his sketchbook; in the other, he still held his pen. Leon had never seen anything like this. No one had.

"Come back!" said Miss Meswania.

But it was too late.

The whole class had already spilled onto the playground. The air outside smelt of static electricity and the sky was still an ominous, otherworldly purple.

"Everyone, stay where you are!" Mr King ran into the playground from his office at the front of the school. He was holding his phone to his ear. "I'm on the phone to the police now."

Suddenly, there was a loud, high-pitched squeaking sound. Leon and Asha covered their ears along with the rest of their class. Then they watched as the base of the spaceship, if that's what it was, suddenly released a cloud of bright green smoke.

"It's farting!" Asif said.

The green smoke smelt of rotten eggs and unwashed football kit. It stank so badly, Leon stopped covering his ears and put his hands over his nose and mouth instead. But it wasn't enough to stop the stench.

He considered running back to the safety of the classroom, but the smoke was so thick, he couldn't see anything.

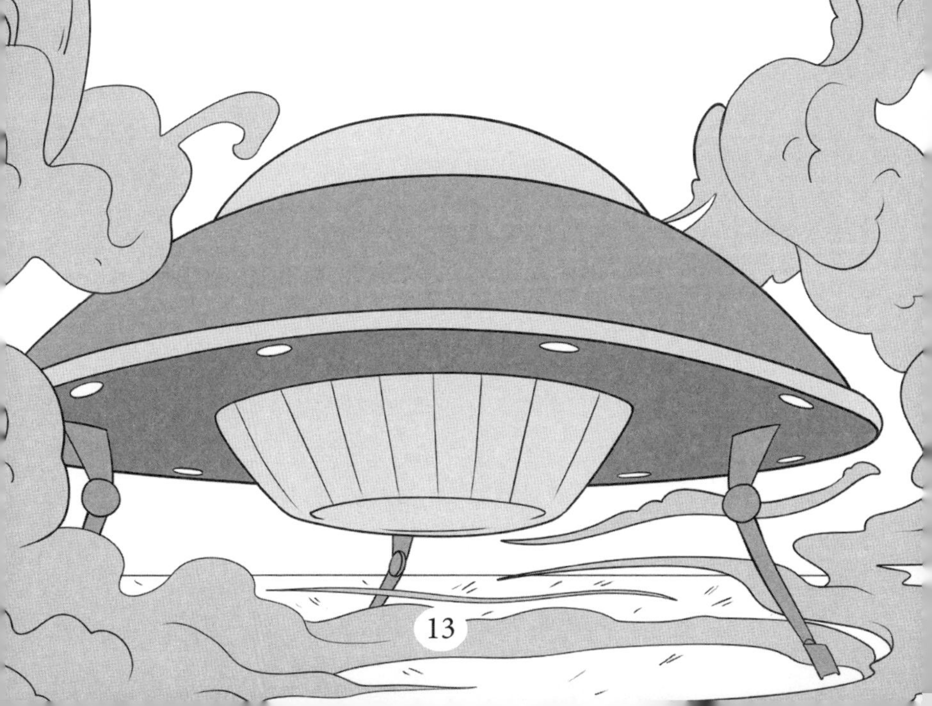

Gradually the smell faded, and the smoke cleared.

When Leon and Asha had both stopped coughing and spluttering, they caught each other's eyes. They were both thinking the same thing – this was like something from one of the graphic novels they loved to read so much. Like the beginning of an alien invasion.

There was silence in the playground as everyone stood and stared at the spaceship to see what would happen next. They didn't have to wait long.

Suddenly, a round hole, roughly half Leon's height, appeared in the metal in front of them. One moment it didn't exist and the next it did. Seconds later, a ramp unfurled from the hole, landing with a gentle bump on the playground in front of Mr King's feet. He jumped back as a dark shape appeared in the hole at the top of the ramp.

Leon and Asha stared, open-mouthed.

Something was coming out of the spaceship, but what?

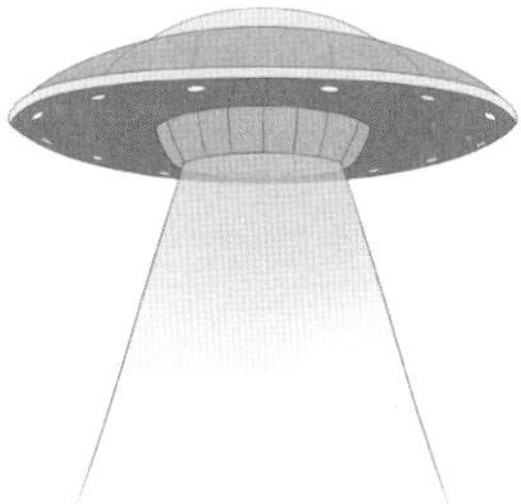

Chapter 3

After a slight pause, a shape moved down the ramp. Leon could only see it clearly once it moved into the slightly purple light. It was quite small, furry-looking and almost completely round. It was followed by a long line of alien creatures who were all the same size and shape as the first. Gradually, they moved in a procession down the ramp until the first one came to an abrupt stop on the ground in front of Mr King's feet.

Everyone leant forwards and tried to get a better look, as the other creatures piled up into the back of the one at the front and knocked it over. Once the first one had straightened up, it started making a series of clicking noises, like it was annoyed.

The other creatures all backed up a little and then the one at the front turned to face Mr King.

The creature came up to Mr King's knees and Leon could see now that it was fluffy all over with two big, black, round eyes in the middle of its body. It was pale pink in colour – the creatures behind it were all different pastel shades of green, yellow, blue and purple.

Leon was itching to capture them on paper. He'd never imagined a creature without a mouth or

arms or legs or ears before. How did it eat? How did it talk?

"Wow! They do *not* look like I expected aliens to look," said Asif.

"They're so cute!" Priya squealed.

"Looks can be deceiving," Asha muttered under her breath to Leon.

The alien in front of Mr King began to click, whistle and purr, as if it was trying to communicate.

"I don't understand," Mr King said, after a moment.

Miss Meswania went to stand beside Mr King. "Hello," she said, smiling at the creatures. "And welcome to Earth!"

The alien slowly shuffled around on the spot until it was facing the one behind it in the line. It clicked and whistled until that alien slowly shuffled round and said something to the one behind it. They kept doing this until they reached the creature at the top of the ramp, closest to the spaceship door, which then moved inside. Then they all froze like they were waiting for something.

"What if they're getting weapons?" asked Asha.

"Stop assuming the worst," Roxy hissed. "Aliens have landed right outside our classroom, which is literally the coolest thing ever, and you're turning it into the apocalypse!"

"I'm just saying, we don't definitely know that they come in peace," Asha mumbled.

"They're way too cute to be evil," Roxy argued.

"We can't know that for sure," said Leon, and Asha shot him a grateful smile.

Finally, the alien at the top of the ramp reappeared. Then it rolled all the way down the ramp until it reached the creature at the front who seemed to be the leader. Out of its side a thick, black arm suddenly appeared. It was holding a small silver button which it pressed into the pale pink fur of the leader. Then the alien's arm disappeared back into its furry body.

"Hello," said the alien at the front of the line,

in a surprisingly booming voice. The small silver button must be a translator. And maybe a megaphone.

Mr King stepped backwards in surprise.

"Hello, Earthlings, we are the Fuzztiks," said the creature. "We come in peace."

"This is so cool!" Asif shouted.

There was a murmur of agreement from the rest of their class.

"Where have you come from?" asked Miss Meswania.

"Our home planet Fuzzball, on the far size of the galaxy."

"Fuzzball? What a rubbish name," Asha whispered to Leon.

"Our planet is in trouble, and we need your help," the alien continued.

"Oh, OK, wow," said Mr King. "Why don't you come to my office so you can tell us everything?" He started walking and the aliens followed behind, some shuffling on unseen feet, others rolling.

Miss Meswania and everyone in their class started to follow them to the front of the school.

"This feels dodgy with a capital D," said Asha, as she tugged on her sister's hand and pulled her back from the crowd.

"Stop overthinking it. They said they need our help." Roxy tugged her hand free. "There's only one way to find out what's going on and that's

to hear what they have to say." She jogged to catch up with everyone else.

Asha was torn between following her sister and listening to her gut. But she hung back and stood with Leon as they watched everyone else go.

After a moment, they were alone in the playground looking up at the alien spaceship. It was hard to believe it was real.

"It isn't the only way," Leon said, after a moment.

"What isn't?" asked Asha.

"To find out what's really going on. We could always go and err ... take a look around." He pointed to the ramp and the spaceship door.

"Leon, are you suggesting that we sneak on board an alien spaceship to see if those cute furry creatures are telling the truth?" Asha put her hands on her hips.

"Yes?" Leon pushed his glasses up his nose. "Maybe it's a bad idea."

"It's definitely a bad idea, but it's the only

way we're going to know for sure if we can trust the Fuzztiks. Let's do it for humankind." Asha grinned and stepped onto the ramp.

Leon took a deep breath and followed her. The ramp felt surprisingly solid beneath their feet as Leon walked up behind her towards the hole in the ship's side.

They had to crouch down on their hands and knees when they reached the small hole. Leon tucked his sketchbook and pen into his pocket.

Asha crawled inside and a moment later, Leon followed her into the spaceship.

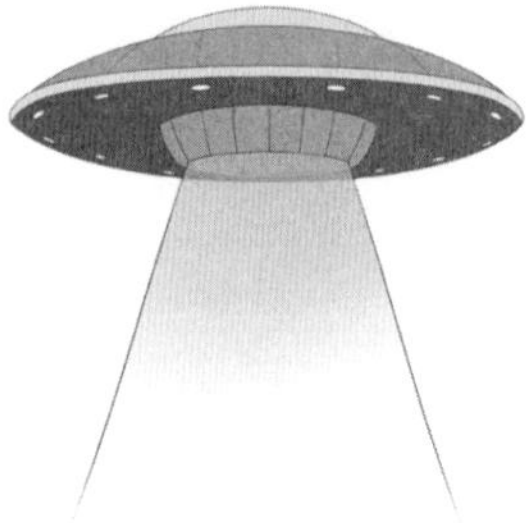

Chapter 4

Inside the ship, the air was much cooler and smelt strangely sweet. Leon could feel goosebumps on his arms and the back of his neck. It took a moment for their eyes to adjust to the dim lighting which came from small spots on the ceiling. Luckily, there was enough room for Leon and Asha to stand up straight.

They were in a curved corridor. Leon ran his hand along one of the pale grey interior walls. It was smooth and cool to the touch.

"What do we do now?" he asked Asha.

"Now, we take a look around," she replied.

They started walking, their footsteps echoing

ominously on the smooth floor, but no aliens came to investigate the sound they made.

"All the Fuzztiks must have disembarked," said Leon.

"Let's hope so," Asha agreed.

They followed the corridor in a gentle curve until they ended up by a small, dark hole in the exterior wall. Leon poked his head through it.

"What can you see?" Asha asked.

"A ramp and our school playground," he replied. "We've walked in a giant circle, haven't we?"

"Looks like it," Asha agreed. "There must be a door or another corridor somewhere that we missed. Let's think like a Fuzztik this time."

"Like a furry alien which may or may not be evil?" Leon asked.

"Like a *small* furry alien," Asha smiled, as she bent down and started crawling along the corridor, stopping every now and again to run her hands up the smooth walls.

Leon bent down and started crawling behind her. It was starting to feel pointless. Then he noticed three tiny black circles in a line, right by the edge of the floor where it met the wall. It was probably nothing, but he pressed the dots anyway and then nearly fell over in shock when a round doorway instantly appeared in the wall.

"Asha," he called, "I've found something."

She scrambled back to him in a rush, and he showed her the dots on the floor.

"Good find!" she smiled. "Now let's see what's inside."

Leon crawled in first this time then stood up, blinking in the bright light. The room was circular with huge, brightly-lit screens filling every wall. Nearer the floor, there were lots of smaller screens with buttons. Some of them were flashing. It looked like some kind of control room.

He stood in the middle, slowly turning around to take it all in, whilst Asha walked around the room.

"Leon, over here," she called.

Leon walked over and looked at the screen she was pointing at. It showed a map of space, with Earth right at the centre surrounded by lots of silver

circles. Leon recognised some of the other planets in their solar system.

"What do you think those circles are?" Leon pointed at the screen.

"They look a bit like this ship," Asha said.

"But why would a load of Fuzztik spaceships be surrounding Earth?"

"They said they needed our help; maybe they're waiting for us to help them somehow?" Asha suggested.

"Maybe," said Leon. Although neither of them sounded convinced.

Leon pulled his sketchbook out of his pocket and quickly drew the image of Earth surrounded by spaceships.

"What if needing help from us is just a cover story?" Asha said. "We need to find out why they're really here." She bent down and started fiddling with the buttons on one of the small screens.

"Are you sure that's a good idea?" Leon

asked, as the big screen started making a weird bleeping noise and more lights on the buttons started flashing.

"It's probably as good an idea as sneaking on board an alien spaceship," Asha said.

"Fair," replied Leon, "unless you launch us into space – "

Suddenly, the screen to the side of them changed to show a series of computer-generated images. The first image was the Fuzztiks arriving on Earth looking cute and friendly. The people in the picture looked happy and excited. When the next image flashed up on the screen, it showed people standing in rows, all staring straight ahead with blank expressions.

The one after that showed people chopping down trees, collecting water, mining stone and loading it into crates. The final image showed hundreds of spaceships, each with rows of humans pushing heavy-looking crates up their ramps and into the ships. The Fuzztiks no longer looked cute.

Their expressions had changed – they looked evil.

"I don't think they do come in peace," Leon said.

"Nope," Asha shook her head. "They're here for resources: our water, wood and stone."

"They're parasites," Leon realised. "They look like cute fuzzy balls but they're actually just – "

"Ticks," Asha finished. "Like the bloodsucking

parasite we found on my cat last week. Only much bigger."

"I don't get why they think we'll just roll over and let them take what they want though?" Leon said, angrily. "They've obviously done enough research to know what we look like and the language we speak; they must know we'll fight back."

"Maybe they don't know as much about humans as they think, or perhaps we're missing something?" Asha started to fiddle with the buttons again, when they both heard a noise.

It sounded like movement in the corridor outside.

"They're back," Leon said, as his heart started to race. "We need to get off this ship before they find us and figure out that we've seen their evil plan."

"Good idea," Asha agreed, "but ... where's the door?"

The door they'd come in through had closed silently whilst they'd been looking at the screens. Neither of them had noticed at the time.

Leon couldn't remember where in the room they'd entered from as it all looked the same. He put his sketchbook and pen back in his pocket.

They both bent down and frantically started scanning the floor for the doorway dots.

"Where are they?" Asha hissed. "Where are they?"

Leon could hear the sounds outside getting louder and louder. They were running out of time.

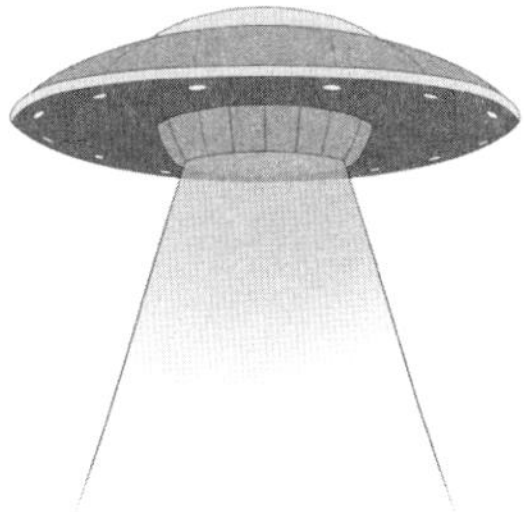

Chapter 5

"There!" Leon pointed.

Asha dived, pressed the dots and rolled through the door that appeared. Leon scrambled after her.

They were back in the smooth, circular corridor that ran around the edge of the ship but the noise of the Fuzztiks approaching was even louder.

They were really close now.

Leon froze. What if the aliens found them? What if they went through their pockets and discovered the map in his sketchbook he'd drawn? They'd know they'd been in their control room.

Asha tugged the sleeve of his jumper and motioned for Leon to follow her. They set off at a fast tiptoe away from the sounds, both being careful not to make any noise.

Leon's eyes began to water, his nose twitched. He just knew he was going to sneeze. He clasped his hands over his mouth and nose and tried to stifle the sneeze, but it didn't work. Asha froze. Behind them, the shuffling sound of the Fuzztiks stopped.

The moment seemed to stretch on forever, then everything sped up.

The noise behind him got louder and in front of him Asha started to run. Leon started running, too. Where was the exit? Surely it couldn't be much further.

Finally, Asha bent down. She'd spotted some more dots on the floor. Leon followed her through the hole that opened in the corridor wall. But instead of landing on the ramp, back in the fresh air like he'd expected, they were somewhere else. In a long, low room which had shelves along each side. Asha pressed the dots so the door closed.

"This isn't the way out!" he whispered.

But Asha frantically shushed him as the sounds got louder and louder until they stopped right outside.

Leon held his breath; he felt sure they were going to be discovered.

Then the sounds moved on, until they faded away completely.

"That was close," Leon said.

"Way too close," Asha agreed.

"We need to go back and find the right door. We've got to get off this ship and warn everyone," Leon said.

"Yeah, but let's stay here for a moment," Asha suggested, "to make sure they've definitely gone."

"What is this place?" Leon wondered, as he turned to look at the shelves in the room. They were full of all kinds of strange items in all shapes and sizes. Some of the objects looked like bits of technology; some looked organic. Asha spotted a few items from Earth: an old cassette player, a wellington boot. Every item had a label below it, not that either of them could read the alien's writing.

"Maybe it's stuff the Fuzztiks have found in space?" Asha wondered, as she walked beside the row of shelves. "Like an alien lost property room?"

But Leon wasn't listening. His eyes had been drawn to a shelf at the back of the room and a tall, thin dark crystal which seemed to be sucking all the light towards it.

"What's that?" he asked, as he walked over and crouched down to take a better look.

It was roughly as big as his hand and as wide as a tennis ball. It was standing upright on a circular silver base.

Leon reached out to pick it up and felt a zing of static electricity as his hand touched one side of the dark crystal. It was warm to the touch and made him feel warm inside his belly too, like he'd just had a hot chocolate or something.

"Look at this," he showed Asha.

"What are you doing?" she shrieked. "Put it back! We're on board an alien spaceship. You can't just go around picking up weird, glowing crystal artefacts! You don't know what will happen!"

"But I'm fine," Leon argued. "It's fine." Although now that he thought about it, it wasn't that normal for crystals to make you feel warm inside, was it?

Leon turned the crystal over in his hands.

He should probably put it back but there was something about it ...

Asha snatched the crystal out of his hands and

yelped as she felt a zing of static electricity, too. She put it firmly back on the shelf.

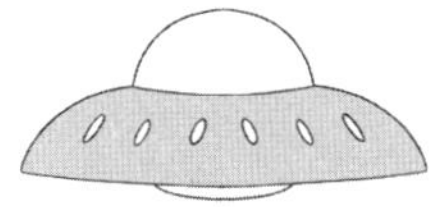

Leon felt the warmth leach of out his body. He was suddenly quite cold. Maybe Asha was right, and it hadn't been a good idea to touch the light-sucking crystal in the alien lost property room.

"Let's go," Leon told her.

But Asha was still standing in front of the shelf she'd put the crystal back onto.

Leon forcefully tugged her away, back over to the door.

She shook her head to clear it. "That was weird."

"Did you feel warm inside, too?" Leon asked.

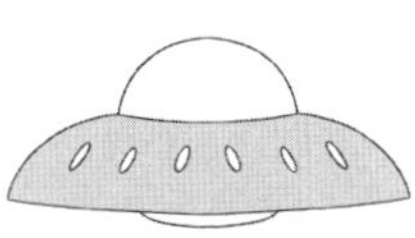

"Yeah, not in a bad way, at least I don't think so," Asha said. "But I feel cold now."

"Me too," Leon said.

They both listened by the door for a moment. It was quiet outside now, but what if it was a trap?

What if the Fuzztiks were waiting for them on the other side of the door?

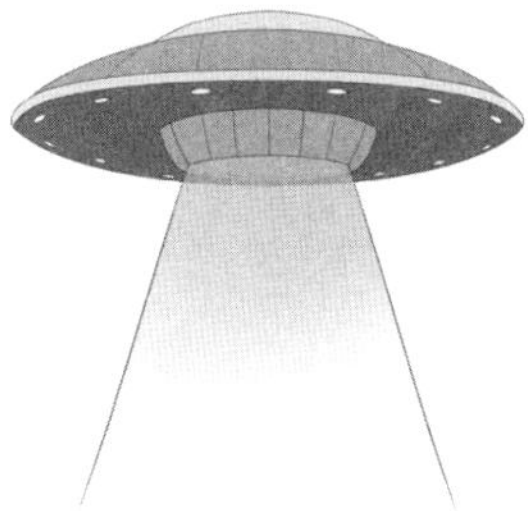

Chapter 6

Asha pressed the dots and they both held their breath as the door opened. Leon peered into the corridor and sighed with relief. The coast was clear.

Together they crept down the corridor, alert for any noise. But there was silence. It felt like they'd been walking for ages when, finally, they spotted more dots on the floor.

"Do you think those are the right dots?" Leon asked.

"Let's find out," Asha said, as she pressed them.

"I never thought I'd be so happy to see our school again," Leon sighed with relief, as the door opened and revealed a glimpse of purple sky and the playground.

Asha and Leon ducked through the small opening and ran down the ramp as fast as they could. They rushed through the playground and into their empty classroom.

They had to find their teachers to warn them! They needed to tell the police and probably the government that there was an armada of alien ships surrounding the planet, waiting to invade and steal all of Earth's resources.

Leon was just about to leave their classroom, when Asha stopped.

"Where *is* everyone?" she asked.

"What do you mean?" Leon furrowed his brow.

"Why isn't everyone back? Where are the teachers? And where are the Fuzztiks?"

It was a good point. Now that he stopped to think about it, Leon realised the school was eerily quiet.

"I can't hear any sirens either," Leon said. "Why

aren't the police here?"

"Yeah, and government helicopters or something. Aliens are kinda a big deal."

"Something's wrong," Leon realised.

"What if we're too late? What if something's happened to everyone? I need to find Roxy." Asha was starting to panic.

"OK, but let's go to Mr King's office to warn him first, then we can look for your sister. I'm sure she's OK. Wouldn't you be able to sense it if something had happened to her, using your twin thing?"

"You know that's not really a thing, right?" Asha took a deep breath. "Right, let's go find the teachers and save the world." She pulled the door open with a bang.

"Yup," Leon nodded, "but let's do it quietly in case the aliens notice, OK?"

"Yeah, let's do that," Asha agreed.

They crept down the corridor. Every classroom

they passed was completely empty. The hairs on the back of Leon's neck stood up. Something was definitely not right.

The closer they got to Mr King's office, the more weirded out Asha and Leon felt. Where was everyone?

Finally, they reached the office. Leon crouched down on the floor and peeked in through the window. Mr King was sitting at his desk and Miss Meswania was standing next to him. He couldn't see any Fuzztiks in the room.

He turned the door handle and beckoned Asha inside. As soon as they were in, they shut the door behind them.

"Sir," Leon said.

"Miss," Asha spoke at the same time.

"The aliens haven't come in peace," Leon said.

"I know they look cute, and they said they're friendly, but they're parasites – ticks. They want to take all of Earth's resources," Asha finished.

There was silence for a moment, and they waited for their teachers to say something, anything. But Mr King and Miss Meswania just stayed exactly where they were, staring into the distance. It was like they hadn't even heard them.

Leon waved his hand in front of their faces. Asha tapped Miss Meswania on the arm. Neither of their teachers even blinked.

"What's happened to them?" Leon asked.

"The Fuzztiks happened to them," Asha

said, her voice trembling with a mix of fear and determination. "I need to find my sister."

"Let's split up," said Leon. "We'll find them faster that way."

"What? Are you joking? That's what people do in books or films before the bad guys get them. We're *not* doing that."

"OK, OK," Leon smiled. Despite the seriousness of the situation, she had a point. "Let's go find our friends."

They opened the door and crept along the corridor towards the hall.

"I can hear something," Asha whispered.

Leon listened. It was the low murmur and shuffling noise you heard during assembly when a large group of kids were having to sit still and were getting bored and fidgety.

They peered through the window in the door to the hall and saw everyone in the school sitting in rows like it was an assembly. Around the side of the hall, the teachers were sitting on chairs. They all had the same, vacant expression that Mr King and Miss Meswania had.

Asha scanned the row of kids for her sister and finally spotted Roxy sitting between Asif and Priya not far from the window. She willed her sister to look at her. Maybe they really *did* have a twin thing because, after a moment, Roxy turned her head towards the window.

Asha waved frantically and tried to beckon her over, but Roxy shook her head slightly. She looked really scared.

"Why isn't she coming?" Asha whispered.

"I think something's happening at the front," Leon said, as a group of Fuzztiks slowly shuffled to the front of the stage. They no longer looked cute. Their eyes now stared at the kids menacingly.

"Let's just go in." Asha stood up. But just as her hand touched the door handle, the Fuzztiks began making a weird high-pitched humming noise.

"What are they doing?" Leon asked.

"I don't know," Asha said, "but I don't think it's anything good."

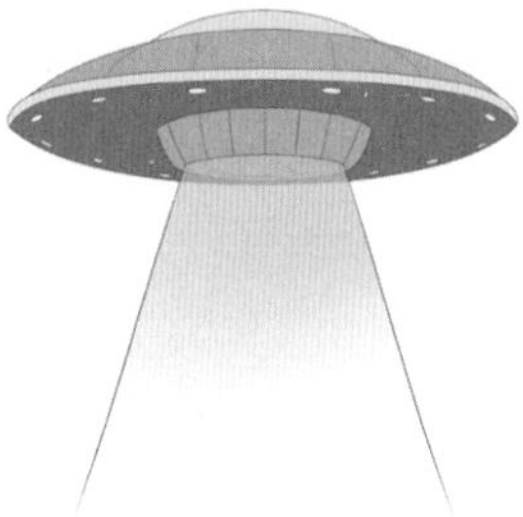

Chapter 7

Asha and Leon watched in horror as the faces of their classmates, friends and Asha's sister Roxy all gradually became as vacant as their teachers. All the shuffling and fidgeting from the kids inside the hall stopped completely.

"No, no, no!" Asha cried.

"Shush," Leon whispered, frantically.

"What have they done to them?" Asha said, in a small voice.

"I don't know, but let's get out of here before they do it to us, too."

"I can't leave my sister," Asha said. "I can't leave Roxy."

“We can’t help them if we get caught, too. Come on.” Leon dragged Asha away from the hall and led her back to their classroom since they knew it was empty. Once they were safely inside, he moved a desk in front of each door to make it harder for anyone to follow them in.

Asha just watched him, shock all over her face.

“It’ll be OK,” Leon said, putting an arm around her shoulder.

“None of this is OK,” Asha replied. “It’s

like something from a film. Or a nightmare."

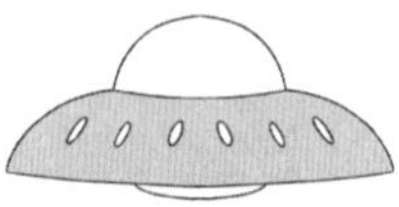

"I know," Leon agreed. "But we're not going to let those parasites get away with it. We're not in a trance like everyone else so it's up to us to stop them."

"Yeah, let's show those evil aliens they can't just take what they want." Asha nodded furiously.

"That's more like it!" Leon punched the air. "Err, how are we going to do that exactly?"

"Let's call the police again," Asha suggested. "Maybe Mr King's call didn't go through?" She picked up Miss Meswania's phone, which was lying on her desk, and dialled. "It's not ringing – it says there's no signal."

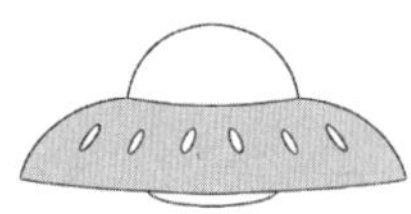

"Maybe there's some kind of a cloaking device over the school, blocking communications?" Leon thought out loud.

"It would explain why no one's come to investigate the giant spaceship sitting in our playground," Asha agreed.

"Let's break out of school and find someone with a working phone," Leon suggested, even though he wasn't totally sure anyone would believe them without proof.

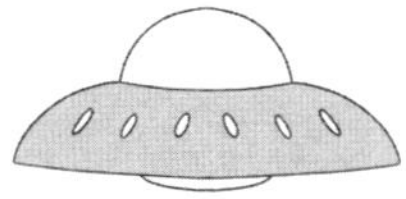

Asha and Leon moved the desk and opened the door that led outside. They ran alongside the playground, keeping as low as possible to avoid being spotted. There was a loose panel in the fence that they could move to one side and squeeze through to get to the footpath. From there, they could knock on the door of the first house they came to and ask to use their phone. But halfway across the field, it felt like they'd run into an invisible brick wall.

"Ow!" said Asha.

Leon and Asha put their hands out to touch it. It was smooth, impossible to see and solid

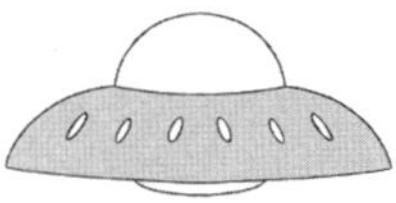

as a rock. Leon bent down, then stretched up, but the invisible wall ran as high and low as he could reach. He followed it for a few steps as it curved gently across the field.

"They must've put a cloaking device *and* a forcefield around the whole school to hide their spaceship from view," Leon said.

Asha put her hands on her hips. "Do you know what, I've had enough of this. This is *our* school. This is *our* planet. Those evil parasitic aliens can't just rock up, put everyone into a trance and steal all of Earth's resources. We're going to take them down."

"Yeah, we are!" Leon whooped. "But, um, how are we going to do that exactly? No one is coming to help us. We're on our own."

"I don't know," Asha admitted. "Let's find out what the aliens are doing, then we can make a plan."

Leon and Asha carefully snuck back into school and crept along the corridors, back to the hall. There were lots of Fuzztiks still inside, but now they were making high-pitched clicks and whistles. One of the Fuzztiks suddenly narrowed its eyes and jumped on one of the others. There was a chomping, slurping sound, and the second alien made an ear-splitting screeching sound. Asha shuddered as purple blood dripped down its fur and onto the wooden floor.

"What are they doing?" Leon whispered.

"Maybe they're arguing about what to do next?" Asha replied. "Which means we have time to stop them. Come on."

"So, about this plan," Leon said, once they were safely back in their classroom with both doors barricaded with desks and chairs. "Where do we start?"

"Let's start with what we know," said Asha. "We know that aliens called Fuzztiks have landed in our school playground. They said they were friendly, but on their spaceship, we discovered plans to steal all of Earth's resources. We don't know how they're going to do that, but we *have* just seen them turn evil and put all the kids in our school into a trance – "

"And all the teachers," Leon added.

"And all the teachers," Asha continued. "I think we can guess that's what they'll do to everyone else."

"What I don't get," said Leon, "is why it didn't work on us? We could hear the noises they were making, too."

"Maybe you have to watch them do it, or we were too far away, I don't know." Asha frowned. "Whatever the reason, we're the only two people who haven't been zombified. We can't use phones to call for help and there's a forcefield around the school so we can't get out. We're on our own."

"So, how do we stop them?" Leon asked. "Could we sabotage their ship?"

"But that would trap them on Earth," Asha pointed out.

"Yeah, you're right. Terrible idea." Leon nodded. "We need them gone, not stuck here forever."

"Can I see the drawings you made of the map and their plans?" Asha asked.

"Sure." Leon reached into his pocket and pulled out his sketchbook. As he flicked through the pages to find the right one, his fingers brushed the drawing he'd done earlier at breaktime of a dragon. All of a sudden, Leon's stomach felt warm inside, like it did when he first touched that black crystal on the ship. The next thing he knew there was a small dragon sitting on the floor next to him. A dragon with razor-sharp teeth and a wicked smile. It sneezed a cloud of smoke at him and grinned.

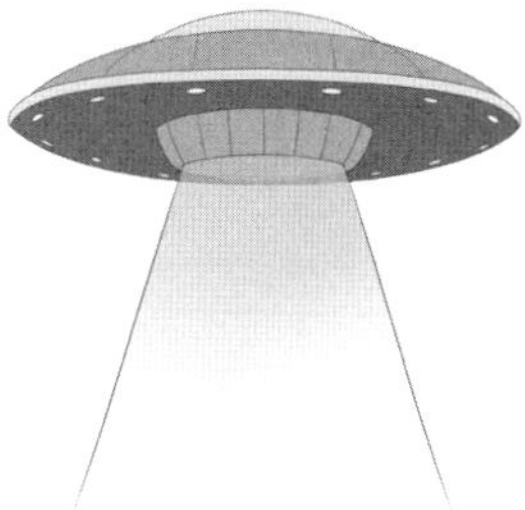

Chapter 8

Leon and Asha scrambled backwards, hearts pounding.

The small dragon casually stretched out its spine and shook out its translucent wings.

"It looks like – " Leon began.

"Dee," Asha said. "The dragon you drew."

Leon looked down at his sketchbook – his drawing from this morning had disappeared. He looked back at the dragon sitting in front of him. "I think my drawing came to life." He stumbled over his words. "But ... how? It makes no sense."

"It makes about as much sense as evil aliens

landing in our school playground," Asha pointed out.

"But there's a dragon, right there. A dragon I drew." Leon stared open-mouthed.

"Hello, Dee," Asha said.

The dragon snorted back.

"I think it can understand us," Asha smiled. "Ask it to do something."

"My drawing is alive. This is so cool!" Leon laughed.

Asha nudged him.

"Oh yeah, right. Hi, Dee," said Leon. "Can you come here, please?"

The dragon tilted its head and casually walked over to Leon. It sat down by his feet and rubbed its head against his shins like a cat wanting a stroke. Leon scratched it behind its ears, and the dragon purred with a low, throaty grumble. It felt surprisingly solid beneath his hands.

"This is amazing!" Asha said. "How did you

bring it to life?"

"I don't know. I didn't mean to do it. I just touched a drawing accidentally, then my stomach felt warm like it did when I touched that dark crystal on the spaceship," Leon replied.

"Try it again with a different drawing," Asha suggested.

Leon flicked through his sketchbook until he found a drawing of a kitten. He touched it, his stomach flickered with warmth again and then there in front of them was a kitten.

The kitten pounced on the dragon's forked tail. The dragon turned round and sneezed more smoke at the kitten, who tumbled backwards and went to hide behind Asha.

"The crystal must have done something to you," Asha said. She scooped up the kitten and it nuzzled into her arms.

"I wonder if it did something to you, too?" Leon thought aloud. "Try and touch a drawing. See if you can bring one to life, too."

Asha put down the kitten and touched one of Leon's drawings.

Nothing happened.

"Maybe it just worked on you?" Asha looked a little disappointed.

"Or maybe it just works differently on you? I'm always drawing but you never draw. You're always – "

"Writing," Asha said. She rushed over to her desk and picked up her notebook of story ideas. She flicked through until she found a short story she'd written about a warrior fairy. She touched it, but nothing happened.

"It's still not working." She shook her head.

"Maybe try reading it?" Leon suggested.

"Once there was a wild warrior fairy called Tiki who lived in the jungle. Her long, brown hair hung in plaits, and she refused to wear dresses. She never went anywhere without her bow and arrow or her trusty knife that she named Razor."

As Asha read her story aloud, she felt the

warm feeling from the crystal spread through her stomach. "I think it's working," she said.

Moments later, a fierce looking fairy stood in front of them. She notched her bow and arrow. "What are we hunting?" she asked.

Asha looked at Leon. "This changes everything."

"Let's see what else we can do!" Leon suggested. "Why don't we see if we can bring a character to life together, like we do when we make graphic novels?"

"Your pictures, my words?" Asha said.

Leon nodded.

"OK, let's try it," Asha said. "How about that tiger from last week?"

Leon flicked through his sketchbook until he found the right page. He touched the drawing as Asha read the words from her notebook.

"Tallulah had lived all her short life in captivity, but she longed to be wild and free. Her burnt orange and black stripes shimmered in the fading light through the bars of her cage."

Seconds later, an enormous tiger appeared before them. She stalked towards them, the muscles in her hide rippling as her eyes narrowed. The kitten scrambled away to hide under a chair.

"Maybe a tiger was a bad choice," squeaked Asha.

"Yup," agreed Leon. "How do we send her back?"

"Maybe I need to read the words backwards?" Asha suggested. They stepped slowly away from the advancing tiger until their backs were against a wall.

Leon gulped.

But Dee and Tiki came to their rescue as Asha started reading. The dragon flew in front of them, stood up on her legs and opened her wings to their full height. Tiki leapt to her side, brandishing Razor in front of her.

The tiger hissed and her ears flattened.

"Try the backwards thing," Leon urged.

The words sounded weird when Asha read them in the wrong order, but apart from that, they didn't do anything.

Dee breathed smoke into the tiger's face.

Tallulah growled, loudly.

"Maybe it's simpler than that?" Leon suggested.

"If you've got an idea, tell me now before Dee sets our classroom on fire or we get eaten by a tiger," Asha said, urgently.

Leon touched the blank sketchbook where Tallulah had been and thought about his drawing returning to the page. Seconds later, she was back in his sketchbook, as if she'd never come to life.

Tiki put down her knife and Dee dropped her wings.

"You did it!" Asha said.

They kept experimenting with Leon's drawings, and used Asha's writing to give purpose to Leon's creations. They also had to make sure that all the things they brought to life knew they were on the same side.

Now that they could create their own team to fight the aliens and had a vague idea of how their powers worked, Asha and Leon started to brainstorm ideas for how to take down the Fuzztiks.

Once they'd worked out a plan, Leon began to draw, and Asha began to write.

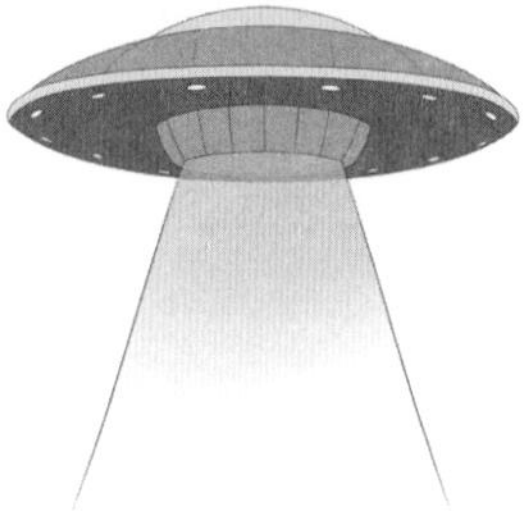

Chapter 9

Leon drew like the fate of Earth depended on it (which it did!) and Asha created more characters than she'd ever thought of before. Her hand ached from all the writing.

Finally, it was done. They were ready.

"You're so amazing at drawing," Asha said, as she flicked through the pages of Leon's sketchbooks.

Leon shrugged. He'd always loved drawing. It came to him easily compared to writing. He'd never be able to write as fast or as neatly as Asha, but perhaps that was OK. It did feel pretty awesome to be able to use his skills to help save the world.

"Are you sure I can't draw characters to just

destroy all the Fuzztiks and smash them into tiny bits or something?" he asked.

Asha shook her head. "We've been over this; we don't want to accidentally hurt any kids or teachers. We need to copy the Fuzztik's strategy – be sneaky and act like we're not a threat so we can get them where we want them. Then we'll strike."

"Yeah, that's a better plan," Leon agreed. "I don't really want to kill them; I just want them to leave us alone."

"So, are we ready for phase one?" Asha asked.

Leon nodded. They unbarricaded the door to the playground and checked it was empty before walking outside.

Leon took a deep breath and began to touch his drawings. One by one, a herd of hastily sketched black and white dragons appeared in front of him, each no bigger than a dog. Beside him, Asha described their characters in detail and gave them their instructions.

"Time to go, dragons," said Leon.

Asha added, “Go, go, go!”

The dragons stretched out their wings and flew in formation over the playground, across

the football pitch, up the ramp and into the belly of the spaceship.

"How will we know if it's working?" Leon asked, chewing the end of his pen.

"I guess we just have to trust that they'll do the jobs we gave them," Asha replied. "Come on, it's time for phase two."

Asha and Leon ran back into their classroom.

"Stay here," Asha told Tiki. "We'll need you later."

They took the barricade down and opened the door to the main corridor.

"Ready?" Leon asked.

"Ready," Asha nodded.

They ran stealthily and quietly along the corridor. But both froze when they saw a Fuzztik moving up ahead. It glanced over them with an evil expression as they stood really still, keeping their faces carefully blank like everyone they'd seen in the hall.

Leon noticed it had purple blood dribbling

down its fur. He held in a shudder, but the Fuzztik didn't even look at them, it just carried on.

Finally, when the sound of the alien moving had faded away, Asha and Leon started creeping along the corridor again.

They kept going until they were back outside the hall. When they peered through the window, all the teachers and kids were right where they'd left them; they hadn't moved at all.

Asha looked at Roxy. She really hoped this plan would work. Her sister was annoying sometimes with all her football chat, but she hated seeing her like this. Like she was hypnotised. She had to save her and everyone else, too.

Leon opened his sketchbook and started touching the drawings he wanted to bring to life. Asha whispered the words she'd so carefully written down in her notebook.

Soon they had ten hand-drawn Fuzztiks standing in front of them. Leon had even taken the time to colour them in. You almost couldn't tell they weren't the real thing.

"Good luck," Leon whispered to them, as he and Asha snuck back out of sight. The fake Fuzztiks opened the door and scuttled into the hall.

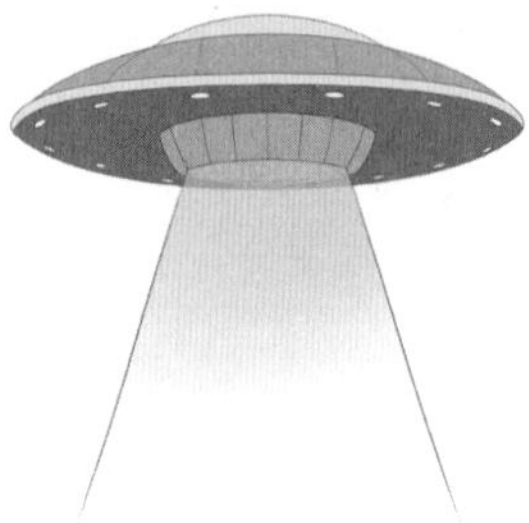

Chapter 10

The fake Fuzztiks went to the front of the hall, barging their way through the other aliens. One fake Fuzztik was holding a hand-drawn radio. He put it down, pressed play and the sound of cheesy pop music filled the hall.

The real Fuzztiks jumped in surprise. They scuttled backwards as the fake Fuzztiks started dancing.

First, the fake Fuzztiks all did different dance moves, some shimmied, some shook, some bounced up and down to the beat.

Then they started to synchronise, all doing the same moves at the same time.

The real Fuzztiks stopped and stared.

Leon briefly wondered if the real Fuzztiks danced or had music on their planet.

A couple of them tried to say something in a series of clicks and whistles, but the fake Fuzztiks just ignored them and kept on dancing.

Another tried to pounce on them, but the fake Fuzztiks shook them off. Asha had written them to be super strong.

"Do you think this will work?" Leon whispered to Asha, as they peered into the hall.

"We're about to find out," said Asha. "Let's go." They crept back along the corridor and hid around the corner, out of sight.

The music got louder as the door to the hall opened with a loud bang. The fake Fuzztiks had started dancing a kind of alien conga, leading the aliens out of the school entrance and towards the spaceship in the playground. Most of the real Fuzztiks were following them.

Asha smiled: their plan was working!

The front door slammed shut so she tiptoed over to the hall to see if there were any aliens left inside.

"Two left," she whispered to Leon. "Let's send in the big guns."

Leon nodded and touched two new drawings to life from his sketchbook.

Asha told them what to do and opened the door so their new creations could sneak inside.

"Meow," went the hand-drawn kittens, as they padded up to the last two Fuzztiks.

The kittens rolled over in front of them, chased their tails and pounced on each other playfully.

The two Fuzztiks moved closer to investigate. They looked really confused.

The kittens meowed again loudly and padded over to the door.

The Fuzztiks followed them and opened the door, before the kittens led them out of the school towards the playground.

"It worked!" said Leon, as he high-fived Asha. He couldn't quite believe it.

"If two kittens can do that, let's see what an army of them can do," Asha said, as she opened her notebook and started reading about a hoard of tiny, angry kittens.

Leon opened his sketchbook and touched drawing after drawing of felines until the corridor around them was overflowing with small cats.

Asha stepped very carefully through the tiny animals so she could open the entrance.

"Kittens," Asha said. The kittens turned to face her. "Attack!"

The kittens poured past her in a wave that flowed towards the playground and the Fuzztiks who'd gathered in front of their spaceship. The fake Fuzztiks were still dancing.

Leon followed Asha outside, then they both paused for a second. Leon touched two new drawings, as Asha read aloud from another page in her notebook.

"Nice dragon," Asha said to Leon, as she climbed onto her large, red, fire-breathing dragon.

"Thanks," he smiled. "Now check out Dee, mark two."

Leon took a deep breath before he climbed up on top of Dee, who was now much bigger than he'd originally drawn her. She also had bigger wings, sharper claws, and a saddle for Leon to sit on.

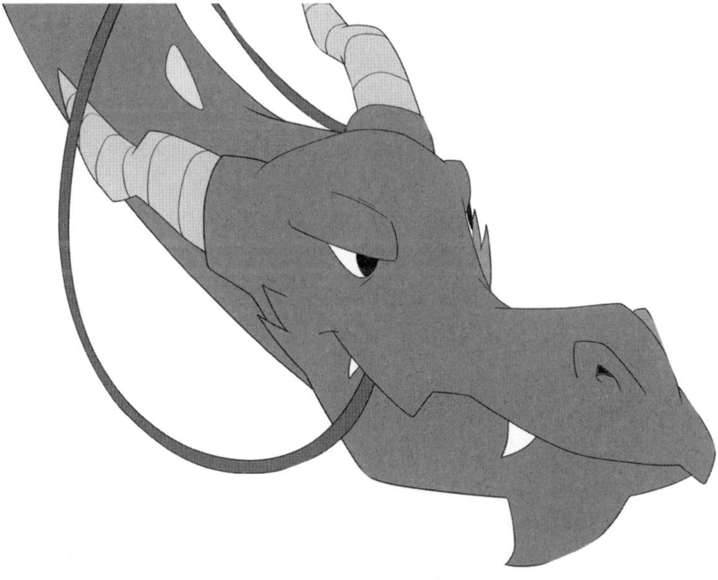

Dee prepared to take flight and Leon gripped onto the saddle with a mixture of excitement and fear. Could hand-drawn dragons fly? Was this plan actually going to work? They really should have tested it out first, but there hadn't been time.

Dee beat her wings, once, twice, and then they were up in the air. Leon felt the air rush past him as he peered over his dragon's shoulder and watched his school get smaller below him.

He urged Dee up higher, just in case the forcefield didn't extend vertically. Perhaps they could fly away and call for help? Perhaps they didn't need to rely on a hastily thrown together plan and made-up characters to save the world?

But Dee squawked in pain as her wings bumped into the invisible barrier above her.

That answered his question.

Leon urged Dee to fly back down to where Asha was hovering over the playground on her dragon.

"What's yours called?" Leon asked, as he flew beside Asha.

“Flame,” Asha smiled. “Because our enemies are toast.”

They watched as their army of kittens surrounded the Fuzztiks. It was time to put the next part of their plan into action.

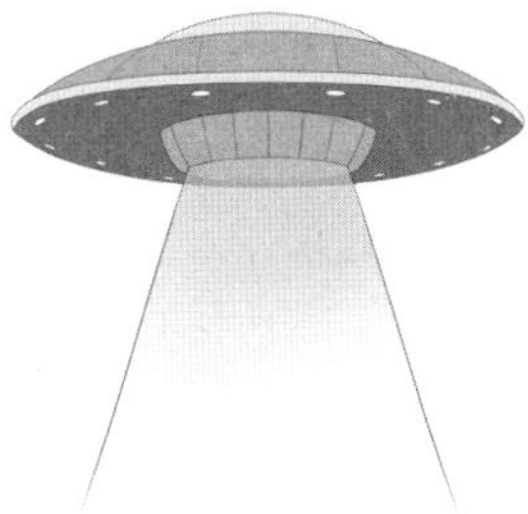

Chapter 11

The kittens were running towards the Fuzztiks and pounced on them with their sharp claws. Some of the aliens had turned and fled back onto their ship, just like Asha and Leon hoped they would.

Some of the other felines were running circles around the Fuzztiks, making them dizzy, before trying to herd them towards the ramp which led into their spacecraft.

But there were still too many Fuzztiks in the playground, even once Leon recalled the fake ones back to his sketchbook.

"We need help," Asha said.

Leon flicked through the pages of his sketchbook

until he found what he was looking for. Then he began to bring the warrior fairies he'd drawn to life. They were all different shapes and sizes, and they were all equipped with a wicked looking sword and shield.

Asha pulled out her notebook and began to read so that they'd know who they were and what they had to do.

Tiki emerged from the classroom and led the warrior fairies. They charged towards the

Fuzztiks, each uttering a battle cry and brandishing their weapons; many of the Fuzztiks turned and scuttled back onto their ship. But some of them stayed and leapt onto the fairies, biting them with pincers which had emerged from somewhere deep within their fur. The fairies howled in rage and attacked with a vengeance, but the Fuzztiks were unstoppable. The fairies they didn't bite, they put into a trance.

Asha flipped to a new page in her notebook and read out a scene where the herd of dragons they'd sent onto the alien spaceship returned to the playground, and helped fight. Perhaps that would turn the tide of the battle in their favour? Hopefully, by now, the dragons would've had enough time to achieve their mission of chewing through wires, melting control systems and, Leon's favourite part, pooing on the Fuzztiks' beds.

Leon asked Dee to fly lower over the playground so he could get a better look at what was going on.

Angry kittens, fierce fairies and tiny dragons all battled to get the Fuzztiks back onto their spaceship. In all the chaos, Asha and Leon couldn't tell who was winning.

A couple of the aliens pointed up to where Leon and Asha were flying on their dragons. Leon watched as they turned their attention towards them.

"Asha, fly up!" he yelled. He told Dee to fly as high as she could.

Asha followed. "What's happening?"

"The Fuzztiks spotted us and if they put us, or our dragons, in a trance, it's game over."

Asha shuddered. "Flying dragons seemed like a great idea at the time but I hadn't thought of that – "

"Me neither," said Leon, as he watched the Fuzztiks hyponotise the remainder of their warrior fairies, kittens and dragons. "What now?"

Their plan wouldn't work unless all the aliens were back on their spaceship, and they had no one left on the ground.

"We need something that doesn't have ears, so it won't get put in a trance, and will be strong enough to pick up the Fuzztiks and put them back on board their ship," Asha said.

Leon thought for a moment. "How about an enormous spider?"

"Eight legs, great idea," Asha said.

Leon started scribbling.

"Good luck," Leon whispered, as he touched the drawing into life and Asha read aloud so it would know what to do.

They watched the spider appear far, far below them in the middle of the playground.

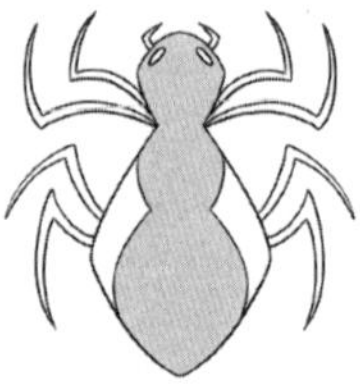

The gigantic spider started shooting white sticky webbing around each of the Fuzztiks.

Some tried to dodge out of the way, others tried to put the spider in a trance, but their weird humming didn't work on it.

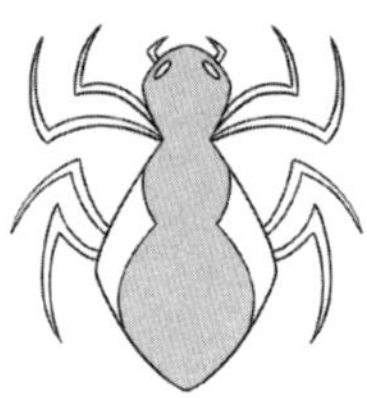

It didn't take the spider long to wrap up the remaining Fuzztiks. They looked like they'd been mummified.

Once the Fuzztiks were all tied up, Asha and Leon flew lower and instructed the spider to pick the aliens up one by one and put them into their ship.

"Goodbye aliens and good riddance," Asha said, as the spider shoved the last one through the doorway of the spaceship.

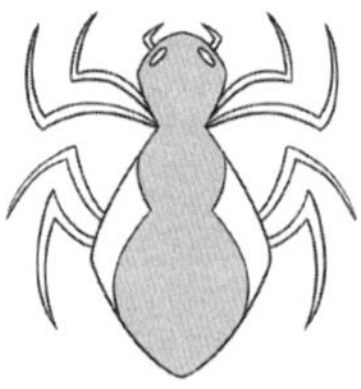

"Do you hear that, Fuzztiks?" Leon shouted. "You're going back to where you came from. This is *our* planet and you're not welcome here. Tell all the other spaceships out there that if you ever come back to Earth, turn humans into zombies and try to take what's ours, we'll destroy you!"

"Bit violent," Asha said.

"Too much?" Leon replied.

"Nah. We don't want them coming back for round two, do we?"

Leon shook his head as he touched his final two drawings to life. Asha read from her notebook and told them what they needed to do. This was it! Their final two creations would end the battle.

"You might want to take down your forcefield, Fuzztiks," Asha said, "or you're going to crash into it."

"Do you think they'll listen?" asked Leon.

Asha shrugged. "I guess we'll find out."

They watched as the giants they'd created

stomped across the playground, making the ground shake with every footstep.

The ramp going into the spaceship quickly retracted and the doorway disappeared a second later.

It seemed the aliens had been listening after all.

The two giants each picked up a side of the spaceship. Then they stood up, holding the ship between them. In one smooth motion, they each stamped a foot to activate their rocket power boots. Then they crouched down for a moment before they blasted up towards the sky, taking the ship with them.

Leon and Asha watched from their dragon's backs as the giants and the spaceship got further and further away, until they disappeared completely.

"Well, the forcefield has gone," said Leon, as they touched down to the ground. "Thank you, Dee," he said.

Asha thanked Flame too, before Leon recalled them both back to the pages of his sketchbook.

“Do you think the trance they put everyone under will have gone, as well?” asked Asha, nervously.

“I hope so,” Leon replied, before realising that all of their creations were still frozen in the playground.

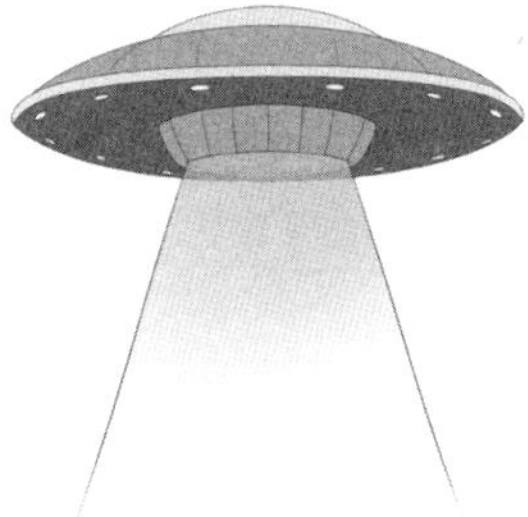

Chapter 12

Leon recalled all the remaining characters and drawings back to his sketchbook. The playground looked strangely empty without them.

Then Leon and Asha ran over to the school entrance. They pulled the doors open and skidded in to the hallway, but they hadn't gone far before they heard a rumble of voices coming from the hall.

Leon and Asha turned to look at each other with a matching hopeful expression on their faces. Had they really done it? Was it all over?

They started running towards the hall only to be stopped by a loud voice. "Asha! Leon! You know we don't run in school." They turned around to see Miss Meswania walking with Mr King out of his office.

"Oh yeah, of course," said Asha, smiling.

"Sorry, Miss!" Leon laughed.

They both walked as fast as they could towards the hall and flung the doors open. They were met with rows of kids chattering and fidgeting.

The teachers around the edge of the hall were scratching their heads like they weren't quite sure what they were doing in there.

Asha and Leon squeezed past some of the kids in their class until they reached their friends. Asha pulled Roxy in for an urgent, tight hug.

"Asha, you can put me down. I saw you like, two seconds ago," Roxy mumbled.

But Asha just held on tighter.

"OK, everyone, silence please." Mr King walked to the front of the hall and held up his hand for quiet. The ripple of chatter slowly faded out. "Now I know this morning has been a bit unusual," he said. Then he looked at his watch. "Oh, my mistake, it's actually the afternoon. Almost time to go home. Right, back to your classrooms everyone."

Asha and Leon glanced at each other as they joined everyone else and began filing out of the room and back to their classroom.

Did Mr King remember any of what had happened? Did he even know that an alien spaceship had landed in their school? Did anyone apart from them remember anything at all?

Back in their classroom, Miss Meswania was just as flustered. “I don’t know where today has gone, or why the tables and chairs are in such a mess,” she said to everyone before she dismissed them. “I’ll see you all tomorrow.”

“Roxy,” Asha asked, as they walked outside, “what do you remember about today?”

“What do you mean, ‘what do I remember’?” Roxy asked, her brows furrowed. “I remember, um. Well.” She frowned.

“Do you remember me beating you at football at break?” Asif said, as he fell into step beside them.

Roxy rolled her eyes. “I remember it hailed, then the sky went purple and then we all got up to look at something, didn’t we?” She looked at Asha for reassurance.

Asha nodded.

"I remember that," said Asif. "Sort of. It's hazy, like it happened a long time ago."

"Or to someone else," Roxy added.

Asif nodded. "Yeah."

There was silence for a bit before Roxy said, "Fancy a kickabout at the park?"

"Go on, then," Asif said. "If you're ready for me to beat you again."

"In your dreams, Asif," Roxy laughed.

"Well, that was weird," Asha said, once Asif and Roxy were busy playing football.

"Which bit? The alien invasion or the fact that no one remembers it." Leon smiled.

"Both I guess."

"Why don't you think any of them can remember anything?" Leon wondered.

"My best guess is that the trance the Fuzztiks put them under wiped their memories," Asha said.

“Do you think our powers stopped when the crystal left too, or do you think that’s different?” Leon wondered.

“I don’t know. I guess we’ll have to test it to find out.” Asha smiled. “Maybe we should wait until we’re not in the park for that though.”

"Agreed." Leon sat back and stretched. "It feels good, doesn't it?"

"What does?" Asha asked.

"Saving the world."

"Yeah, it does. Even if no one remembers it but us," Asha said. "Actually, that gives me an idea – "

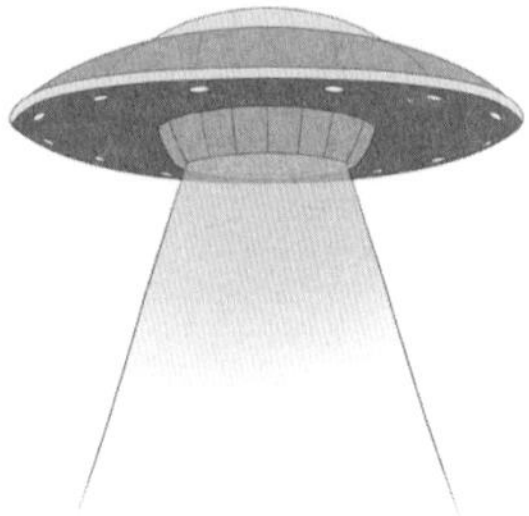

Chapter 13

A couple of months later, Leon and Asha stood up in front of their class. They'd asked Miss Meswania if they could share the new graphic novel they'd made.

"What's it called?" Miss Meswania asked.

"*Evil Fuzzy Aliens vs Kittens With Claws*," Leon said.

"Hmm, sounds interesting," said Miss Meswania, as Asha began to explain what the story was about.

"So, one day a spaceship full of aliens called Fuzztiks lands in this perfectly ordinary school."

"They're so cute," said Priya, as Asha showed everyone the artwork.

"I think they're creepy," said Roxy, with a shudder.

"What happens next?" asked Asif.

"Well, the Fuzztiks say they come in peace, and everyone believes them apart from two kids, Jack and Tia," Leon explained.

"The Fuzztiks lead all the kids and teachers inside where they put them in a trance. Meanwhile, Jack and Tia sneak on board the spaceship where they discover the aliens are evil," Asha said.

"And they find a crystal that gives them powers," Leon added.

"What happens after that?" Priya asked.

"You'll have to read it and find out," said Asha, with a smile.

"Well," said Miss Meswania, "what an incredible imagination you both have. These drawings are fantastic, too."

"You have no idea," whispered Asha to Leon, under her breath.

At breaktime, no one wanted to play football. They all wanted to read *Evil Fuzzy Aliens vs Kittens With Claws* instead.

"Do you think a tiny part of them does remember?" wondered Leon.

"Maybe," said Asha.

"And you're sure we can't tell them the truth?" Leon asked.

Asha shook her head. "I don't think anyone would believe us."

"We could show them our powers?" Leon suggested.

Both Asha and Leon had been ecstatic to discover that their powers hadn't disappeared with the aliens. They weren't sure how long their powers would last, but they were determined to make the most of them while they had them.

"You need to read more books," Asha said. "If we show anyone our powers, then someone from the government will take us to some secret lab and experiment on us."

"They might not," Leon argued. "Besides, shouldn't we warn the government in case the Fuzztiks come back?"

"We could send them a copy of our graphic novel?" Asha suggested.

Leon smiled. "Let's do it."

"The Fuzztiks better *not* come back," growled

Asha. "But we should make sure we're ready for them, just in case."

"OK," agreed Leon. "I'm going to need a bigger sketchbook, and maybe some new pens."

"Yes," said Asha, "you are. I'll need a new notebook, too."

"Maybe we should come up with a superhero team name?" Leon suggested. "And a logo?"

"Like what?" asked Asha.

"What about the Dangerous Doodles, or the Creative Duo, or the Sketch Wizards?" he suggested.

"Hmm. We can work on that," said Asha. "We've got plenty of time now that we don't have an alien invasion to stop."

Book talk questions

What makes Leon and Asha such a dynamic duo?

How does Leon's ability to bring drawings to life help in their fight against the aliens?

Why do you think the aliens choose to invade Earth in the first place?

What does the story teach us about how to react in an emergency?

What other storybook characters would work well in a team with Leon and Asha?

If you had Leon's power, what would you draw to help you in a crisis?

What does the story teach about responsibility and using your powers for good?

How does Leon grow throughout the story as a character?

What was the scariest moment during the alien invasion?

How does the friendship between Leon and Asha help them overcome challenges?

Ask the author

What would be your superpower to fight an alien invasion?

I read really quickly but I'm not sure that would help me battle aliens. Maybe telekenesis, the power to move things with my mind, would be more helpful. I could simply move the aliens *and* it would be helpful when I wanted something just out of reach.

Naomi Jones

Which character do you most identify with?

Probably Asha as I love writing stories and making up characters too.

How did you first get into writing?

I loved reading stories and playing make believe games when I was a kid. I first remember writing stories at school and I loved that I got to let my imagination go wild. I still love the feeling of starting a story and finding out where it goes as I write it.

What was your inspiration for *Leon and Asha vs the Aliens*?

I get my ideas from loads of places. I was picking

my kids up from school and as we walked across the playground I suddenly thought, "I wonder what would happen if an alien spaceship landed now?" My boys also both love drawing comics and graphic novels and I've always thought how cool it would be if their drawings came to life.

How did you come up with the setting for the book?

When you're a kid you spend loads of your time in school. I get to visit lots of schools across the country when I do author visits and they're all different, but they all have similarities too, like a playground.

What was your favourite book as a child?

There are so many books I loved that it's hard to choose just one. *Northern Lights* by Phillip Pullman was definitely one of my favourites though – I still love it now.

Who would you most want to be paired with if you had to fight an alien invasion?

Wonder Woman or maybe Captain Marvel – they're both pretty fierce!

Collins
BIG CAT

Published by Collins
An imprint of HarperCollins*Publishers*

The News Building
1 London Bridge Street
London SE1 9GF
UK

Macken House
39/40 Mayor Street Upper
Dublin 1
D01 C9W8
Ireland

10 9 8 7 6 5 4 3 2 1

ISBN 978-0-00-874478-6

British Library Cataloguing-in-Publication Data
A catalogue record for this publication is available from the British Library.

Author: Naomi Jones
Illustrator: Leo Trinidad (The Bright Agency)
Publisher: Laura White
Commissioning editor: Holly Woolnough
Development editor: Zoë Clarke
Product manager: Holly Woolnough
Content editor: Selin Akca
Copyeditor: Sally Byford
Proofreader: Catherine Dakin
Reviewer: Lisa Davis
Cover designer: Sarah Finan
Internal design: 2Hoots Publishing Services Ltd
Typesetter: Jouve India Ltd
Production controller: Katharine Willard
p108 © John Hersey

Collins would like to thank the teachers and children at Grange Primary School, Southwark, for being part of the development of Big Cat Read On.

Printed in the UK.

FSC www.fsc.org
MIX
Paper | Supporting responsible forestry
FSC™ C007454

This book contains FSC™ certified paper and other controlled sources to ensure responsible forest management.

For more information visit: www.harpercollins.co.uk/green

Made with responsibly sourced paper and vegetable ink

Scan to see how we are reducing our environmental impact.